# Will Too Many Pets Ruin Pets, Inc.?

"Umm," Tina began finally. "Is there something—special about it I need to know? I mean is it valuable, or sick, or something?"

Mrs. Tendyke glanced up. "It?" she repeated. She gave Tina a strange look.

"The rabbit," Tina said.

"The rabbit? *Bugsy*?" Mrs. Tendyke laughed. She opened the back door. "Don't worry about him. He takes care of himself. Girls! Come on inside!"

Now it was Tina's turn to give Mrs. Tendyke a strange look. "Then what do you want me to do?" she asked.

"What do I"—Mrs. Tendyke broke off as two little red-haired girls came through the door. Mrs. Tendyke put a hand on each of their heads. "Just normal baby-sitting," she said. "Nothing special."

Tina felt her eyes widen. She stared at the two little girls. Someone had made a big mistake. She was a pet-sitter, not a baby-sitter!

# TOO MANY PETS

## Jennifer Armstrong

A BANTAM SKYLARK BOOK®
NEW YORK · TORONTO · LONDON · SYDNEY · AUCKLAND

TOO MANY PETS
A Bantam Skylark Book / June 1990

Skylark Books is a registered trademark of Bantam Books, a division of
Bantam Doubleday Dell Publishing Group, Inc. Registered in U.S. Patent
and Trademark Office and elsewhere.

Produced by Daniel Weiss Associates, Inc.
33 West 17th Street
New York, NY 10011

PETS, INC. is a trademark of Daniel Weiss Associates, Inc.

ISBN 0-553-15804-X

Published simultaneously in the United States and Canada

Bantam Books are published by Bantam Books, a division of Bantam
Doubleday Dell Publishing Group, Inc. Its trademark, consisting of the
words "Bantam Books" and the portrayal of a rooster, is Registered in U.S.
Patent and Trademark Office and in other countries. Marca Registrada.
Bantam Books, 666 Fifth Avenue, New York, New York 10103.

PRINTED IN THE UNITED STATES OF AMERICA

OPM    0  9  8  7  6  5  4  3  2  1

# 1

Jenny Sawyer flipped her blond braid over her shoulder and picked up two index cards. "Okay everyone, here are our customers for today," she said. "Mrs. Archer and Mrs. Mead."

Her younger sister, Carrie, groaned. "Mrs. Mead! Attack of the killer geese," she muttered. She leaned her forehead on the kitchen table. "No way am I going to Mrs. Mead's."

"Mrs. Mead's geese have never attacked me," Hilary Burr put in. "You're the only one they ambush."

Tina Martell put down her pencil. She had been trying to sketch Carrie and Jenny's new puppy, Caledonia. But Caledonia never stayed in one place long enough. Drawing her was just about impossible.

"Maybe there's something about you the geese just don't like," Tina suggested. Her brown eyes twinkled behind her glasses. "Animals have a way of knowing things people don't."

Carrie stuck out her tongue at her best friend. "Har-di-har-har, Tina."

Caledonia looked from Carrie to Tina and let out an excited yip.

Tina giggled and picked up her pencil again. The Pets, Inc., Saturday morning business meetings were always fun. Pets, Inc., was the name of the four girls' business. They handled almost every kind of pet-related job, from dog walking to birdseed buying, fishtank cleaning to cat feeding.

Pets, Inc., had been in business for a month or so. It had all started when Carrie Sawyer, who was nine, and her sister Jenny, who was one year older, had decided they wanted to buy Caledonia, the fluffy Shetland sheepdog puppy who'd won their hearts. The problem had been convincing their parents that they were mature enough to handle the responsibility of owning a puppy and paying all its expenses too. Since the sisters already did some pet-sitting jobs in the neighborhood, they had decided to try to get even more jobs.

As soon as Carrie and Jenny had filled their best friends in on the plan, Tina and Hilary had jumped right in. How could they *not* help? They were as crazy about animals as Carrie and Jenny were. Carrie and Jenny had brought Caledonia home, but the business was still going full blast. It was officially called Pets, Incorporated, and it was the only business run by kids at Indian Springs Elementary School. The girls now had a long list of customers.

"Well, I'm sorry," Carrie huffed. "But I just can't go to Mrs. Mead's. I don't know why her geese hate me so much. All I know is that every time I go over to muck out Agnes's pen, they try to peck me." Agnes was Mrs. Mead's pet sheep.

Jenny made a check mark on one of the index cards. "Okay, okay. Hilary and I can go there, and Tina and Carrie will go to Mrs. Archer's." She tucked the card back into the blue filing box where they kept all the important information about their clients. As president of Pets, Inc., Jenny took the business very seriously. She was serious about animals, too. She planned to be a veterinarian when she grew up.

"Going to Mrs. Archer's is okay with me," Tina agreed. She glanced at Carrie. "Right?"

Carrie made a face. "Yeah. But she's going to make us late again," she warned.

Tina rolled her pencil between her fingers. Mrs. Archer was a sweet, friendly old lady with two cute dogs named Napoleon and Josephine. Because she had broken her ankle, Mrs. Archer was having the girls come give the dogs a bath every week. All of the members of Pets, Inc., really liked Mrs. Archer. But there was one problem. Mrs. Archer liked to talk. She liked to talk a *lot*.

Secretly, Tina thought Mrs. Archer was just lonely. That made it harder to say no when she wanted them to stay and talk after their job was finished. But they were getting more customers all the time, and sometimes staying too long at Mrs. Archer's caused trouble.

"Just make sure you leave when you're done that's all," Jenny said.

Tina and Carrie looked at each other. Carrie rolled her eyes.

"We should go pretty soon, Carrie," Tina said. She didn't like to keep customers waiting.

Jenny put away the blue file box. Meanwhile, Hilary stood up and brushed herself off. She was wearing her riding

3

clothes. Her family owned a lot of horses, and Hilary spent most of her free time hanging around the stables.

"Do you guys want to eat lunch here?" Jenny asked Hilary and Tina. "We didn't get to cover everything in this meeting, and we could finish up over lunch."

Hilary shrugged. "Sure."

"Say yes, Teen," Carrie commanded. She scowled fiercely at Tina.

Tina tried not to giggle. "Yes, sir!"

"Okay. Let's go!" Carrie scrambled to her feet and headed for the door. "We'll meet you two back here at lunchtime."

Caledonia barked wildly and leapt in the air. The Sawyers' two cats, Squeaky Hinge and Gilligan Potato Chip, popped out from behind a kitchen cabinet and raced into the hall. Just then the phone started ringing.

"Hello?" Jenny shouted into the phone. "Stop barking, Caledonia!" It was so noisy, she wanted to put her hands over her ears. Sometimes the Sawyers' house was like a zoo!

Carrie and Tina ran down the driveway and got on their bikes. The pair headed down Lincoln Avenue. Tina tried to think of a polite way to tell Mrs. Archer they couldn't stay and talk when the job was finished. It made her cheeks hot to imagine doing it.

"Hey!" Carrie yelped. "That's Mrs. Yates's cat." She pointed to a big, gray-striped cat walking down the sidewalk ahead of them.

Tina braked. "Who's Mrs. Yates?"

"You know," Carrie said. "She lives over on the other side of Fountain Park. I've fed her cat a few times. His name is Oscar."

"What's he doing over here?" Tina asked. She looked at the cat again. He was trotting along the sidewalk.

Carrie shrugged. "I don't know. But we'd better take him home."

"Are you sure it's Oscar?" Tina glanced at her watch. "We're going to be late for Mrs. Archer."

"Positive. Come on!"

Carrie shot ahead, and Tina rode after her. When they were just a few feet away from Oscar, Carrie held up her hand.

"Stop," she whispered hoarsely. "Don't scare him."

Both girls set down their bikes and sneaked up on Oscar. Tina ran in front of him while Carrie tiptoed right up behind him. But just as they had him cornered, the cat jumped in the air with all four legs straight out, and his tail puffed out like a feather duster. He took one look over his shoulder and ran off.

"Oh, no! Tina, come on!"

Tina made a face. She had a bad feeling about it. But she didn't want to let Carrie down. She sighed and ran after her friend.

"He went through those bushes," Carrie said. She crouched down and started pushing into some shrubs. "Come on, Teen."

A branch snapped in Tina's face. She swatted at it. "Are you positive it's Oscar?" she asked again. "It could be another cat that looks just like him."

Tina knew it was easy to make a mistake when it came to animals. Her mother had two little Shih Tzus, and those dogs looked exactly the same at first glance. But when Tina

drew them, she saw lots of tiny differences most people would never notice.

Carrie stopped and turned around. "If it's not Oscar, I'll give you the bag of M&M's I've been saving," Carrie promised. Her eyes were wide and serious. There was a leaf stuck in her hair. "But I guarantee it's him."

"Okay," Tina said with a shrug.

They struggled through the leaves until they came out in someone's backyard. Tina looked toward the house. "We should go," she told Carrie in a worried voice. "Come on."

"No—wait! He's up there!" Carrie jumped up and ran toward a big maple tree in the middle of the lawn.

Tina's stomach swooped inside her. She glanced up at the house again, then started crawling across the grass. Carrie was already halfway up the tree.

"I hate this," Tina whispered.

She tiptoed after Carrie until she was right under the maple tree. The branches above her creaked under Carrie's weight.

"Hurry up!" she called softly.

Carrie shinnied along a branch toward the cat. He made his eyes into slits and stared at her, twitching his tail. Then he began to hiss.

"Come on, Oscar," Carrie coaxed. "Come on." She inched along until she could grab the scruff of his neck. Oscar dug his claws into the wood and hissed some more. Carrie kept pulling until he let go.

"Got him!" she whooped. Slowly, she started backing up. Clutching the cat against her chest, Carrie dropped to the ground.

"Let's get out of here," Tina begged.

7

She started running across the lawn toward the bushes. Carrie raced after her, keeping a tight grip on the struggling Oscar.

"Let's put him in my basket," Tina said when they finally got out to the street again. She opened the wicker basket on her bike. She used to think it was old-fashioned, but now she was glad she had it.

Oscar wriggled around like crazy. Finally, the top was buckled down safely. "Okay. Let's go," Tina gasped.

"Mrs. Yates is going to be so surprised," Carrie said happily.

Tina didn't answer. She was concentrating on keeping her balance. Oscar was still trying to get out. He kept banging against the side of the basket, making her bike wobble. They took a shortcut through the park, and turned up Wedgewood Drive. At last, Carrie stopped in front of a big, modern house.

"Here. I'll take him," she said with a grin.

Tina didn't argue. She was just glad to get rid of Oscar. She held her bike up while Carrie unfastened the buckles on the basket and took out the cat. His hair stuck out in all directions, and his tail swished sharply from side to side.

"He's pretty upset," Tina pointed out. "Be careful."

Carrie nodded. "I will." She lifted him by the scruff of the neck and clasped him tightly in her arms. Then she marched up to the front door and rang the doorbell with her elbow.

After a moment, a woman opened the door. "Hi, Carrie," she said. When she saw the cat in Carrie's arms, she looked surprised. "What . . . ?"

"We found Oscar all the way over on Lincoln Avenue," Carrie explained proudly. She held out the cat.

Just then, Tina noticed a movement by Mrs. Yates's ankles. It was a big, gray-striped cat.

"Uh-oh," she whispered.

"But Carrie, Oscar's right here," Mrs. Yates said.

"But—" Carrie gulped, and looked at the cat in her arms. Then she looked at the real Oscar, who was poking his head out the door. The cat in her arms looked at Oscar, too, and let out a low growl.

"Whoops," Carrie said, clapping a hand over her mouth.

"I think you should take that cat back where you found it," Mrs. Yates suggested.

Carrie's face was bright red. "Yes. Um, sorry." She turned and hurried back to Tina.

"I thought you said you were positive," Tina said.

"I . . . I thought I was," Carrie stammered. She placed the angry cat back in Tina's basket. Then they rode back to Lincoln Avenue.

Tina didn't say a word. For one thing, the cat was lurching around in the basket again, and she had to fight to keep her balance. For another, she didn't know what to say. Tina had known it was a bad idea. She'd had a feeling the cat wasn't Oscar. But it was always hard to say no to Carrie Sawyer.

They reached the clump of bushes near where they had caught the imposter Oscar. Tina looked silently at Carrie and undid the buckles. Instantly, the cat popped out and dashed away through the bushes.

"That house is probably where he lives," Tina said in a quiet voice. She avoided meeting Carrie's eyes.

Carrie let out a small sigh. "Sorry."

"Yeah, well. Forget it." Tina made herself smile. "I guess it's kind of funny, when you think about it."

"You really think so?" Carrie looked unsure.

Tina grinned. "Yeah. But now we're really late. We should get going. Oh, and don't forget," she added.

Carrie looked at her. "What?"

"You owe me those M&M's." Tina giggled and pushed off.

# 2

As soon as Tina rang Mrs. Archer's doorbell, excited barking started up inside.

"Listen to Napoleon and Josephine," Carrie whispered. "They'll be glad to see us."

It seemed as if they waited on the porch for a long time. Mrs. Archer had to walk slowly because of her crutches. Finally, the door swung open. "Hello! Good morning!" sang out Mrs. Archer. She gave them both a twinkly smile.

"Hi," both girls said at the same time.

Mrs. Archer's two corgis charged out onto the porch. They were pudgy, and they had short, stumpy legs. Wiggling all over, they sniffed at Carrie and Tina.

"Hi, Polie. Hi, Josie," Tina said. She went down on one knee.

The dogs were wagging their little, stubby tails so fast they looked like a blur, especially when Tina took off her glasses. Then the dogs sniffed her eyes.

"Isn't it weird how they always do that?" Carrie wondered

11

out loud. She knelt down so they could smell her eyes, too. She also held out her hands to them. Both dogs were quivering with excitement.

"Our dogs do it, too," Tina said.

Carrie stood up. "I bet Jenny would try to pretend she knew exactly why."

"It's just their way of identifying you," Mrs. Archer said. She chuckled. "I'm afraid it's bathtime, you little beasts," she told the dogs affectionately.

"Same as usual?" Carrie asked.

"That's right! Into the tub!" Mrs. Archer said.

Tina and Carrie each picked up one of the dogs and headed for the downstairs bathroom. Polie began to whimper.

"You baby," Tina whispered, rubbing her cheek against his soft head. The corgis always made a fuss about taking baths, but once they were in the tub, they settled right down.

"Come into the kitchen when you're done!" Mrs. Archer called as she left them. "I have something to show you!"

Tina and Carrie exchanged worried glances. They listened to Mrs. Archer thumping away down the hall.

Carrie turned on the faucets and lowered her voice. "What do you think we should do?" she asked.

"I don't know . . ." Tina whispered back. She scooped water into a cup and poured it over Josie's back. Josephine looked up with a sad expression in her eyes. Water dripped from her short, bristly hair.

"Good girl," Tina murmured. She trickled soap along the corgi's back and handed the dog shampoo to Carrie. Then she started sudsing.

"Whatever happens, we can't stay late today," Carrie said. She bit her lower lip. "Remember what we said? We just have to leave right after we're finished. Jenny's expecting us at this meeting. And if we don't tell Mrs. Archer . . ."

Tina wrinkled her nose. "If we don't, she'll want us to stay and talk. I know we can't, but I feel so bad when we have to leave Mrs. Archer."

Carrie sighed. "I know."

Tina's cheeks burned. "You'd better tell her."

"I'm not telling her! You tell her!"

"No! I *can't!* Seriously." Tina's voice cracked, and her throat felt tight. "Carrie, you have to tell her, okay?"

Carrie blew a wisp of blond hair out of her eyes. "Well . . . Okay. I'll try."

Tina sighed with relief. "Thanks."

Carrie reached over and turned the faucets on again to rinse the corgis. Tina poured a cupful of water over Josie's back. She stared down at the shivering dog.

"Hey, you know what I found yesterday?" Carrie said brightly. Once Carrie had decided what to do about a problem, she didn't let it bother her anymore.

Tina tried to smile. "What?"

"A garter snake with its skin half off." Carrie's eyes crinkled at the edges as she remembered. "It was so cool!"

Tina's smile got a little smaller. She was afraid of snakes, but she would never admit it to Carrie. "Did you keep it?"

"Yup. But then I had to let it go in the backyard after dinner. Mom didn't want it in the house."

Carrie wasn't afraid of anything. She was always the first one to jump into a new situation. And she was always the first one to adopt any slimy, furry, scaly, or feathery animal in sight.

Tina picked up one of the dogs' towels and wrapped it around Josie. "Ready?" she asked.

"Yeah." Carrie bundled up Polie, and they gave both dogs a brisk rubdown.

The girls looked at each other when they heard Mrs. Archer coming toward the bathroom.

"You'll tell her, right?" Tina whispered.

Carrie gulped. "I'll try."

"Yoo-hoo!" The bathroom door opened, and Mrs. Archer peeked in. "I've got something special to show you girls," she announced. "Bring the dogs into the kitchen to dry off."

Tina's smile felt stuck on her face. How could they just walk out on such a friendly old lady? She swallowed hard and glanced at Carrie.

Carrie didn't meet Tina's eyes. Her cheeks had turned bright pink.

Tina was looking at Carrie, and Carrie looked at Mrs. Archer. Then Carrie nodded. "Okay," she agreed in a choked voice.

"Come along, then!" Mrs. Archer said cheerfully. She slowly backed out of the bathroom on her crutches. "You're going to love the chocolate cake I baked this morning."

Tina and Carrie shared a helpless glance and giggled. There was always time for cake. Even before they had their lunch.

Tina and Carrie sped down the street. It felt good to ride fast against the wind, Tina thought. They zigzagged down a side street, turned another corner, headed down Lincoln

Avenue, and rattled going up the Sawyers' driveway. A white station wagon with red lettering was parked by the house. It was the Cakemobile, as Carrie called it.

"My mom's home," Carrie observed.

Mrs. Sawyer ran a dessert catering business from their house. It was called Never Desert Dessert. That was what was written on her car. The car also had "Caution Please: Fancy Cake on Board" written in big red script on the tailgate.

Caledonia started bouncing up and down when Carrie and Tina walked into the kitchen.

"You guys are really late!" Jenny announced. She and Hilary were sitting at the kitchen table. In front of them were a pie plate of burned dough and a jar of strawberry jam.

"Gee, thanks for telling us." Carrie made a face and slouched into a chair. She ruffled Caledonia's ears.

"Where were you guys, anyway?" Jenny asked impatiently.

Tina pulled out a chair and sat down. "Guess," she said glumly.

"At Mrs. Archer's? This whole time?" Hilary asked.

Tina nodded. She had a feeling it would be better not to mention the catnapping affair. "Yup," she said. "She made a cake just for us. But then she talked forever. We just couldn't eat and run."

Caledonia came up and licked Tina's hand. Tina reached down and scratched a spot just above the puppy's tail. Caledonia looked up at her adoringly. "Right," Tina added. "So we ate and rode."

15

Hilary laughed and scooped some jam onto a triangular piece of dough. It made a loud crunch when she bit into it.

"What is that?" Tina asked.

Jenny glanced nervously at the door to the hall. "Pie crust," she whispered. She made a face. "Mom burned it while she was taking this really long message for us."

"Oh, no." Carrie grimaced and slumped deeper in her chair.

"Yeah," Hilary put in. "I think she was kind of upset."

"I'll bet she had a total attack," Carrie muttered. Reaching for a piece of pie crust, she added, "So, where were you guys when this happened?"

Jenny's cheeks went pink. "We just got back a little while ago. The geese trapped us in the barn and wouldn't let us out."

Carrie giggled, but then stopped quickly. Tina took off her glasses and polished the lenses with her shirttail. Hilary and Jenny both sighed. They were all thinking the same thing. Most of the Pets, Inc., phone calls came to the Sawyers' house. Mrs. Sawyer was sick and tired of answering the phone while she was busy baking and decorating cakes. She said it was interfering with her business.

"Well, how are we supposed to have a business if people can't call us?" Carrie finally burst out.

"I don't know," Jenny said. "But Mom is really getting mad about it. She says she depends on the phone for her business, too. I guess she thinks we're hogging it."

"We need a secretary and our own phone," Tina said.

"Hey! That's a great idea!" Carrie gasped. "We could have an office somewhere—"

"Forget it." Hilary shook her head. She was the Pets, Inc.,

16

treasurer. "We only have about five dollars for business expenses. That's nowhere near enough."

Carrie slumped down in her chair again. "Nice try," she muttered to Tina.

"Hey, sorry," Tina said. She sighed and put her glasses back on. "But look at the positive side," she went on. "We get a lot of phone calls, and that means we're getting a lot of jobs."

"I know I'll mess up one of these days," Carrie put in gloomily. "It gets so confusing."

Jenny shook her head. "That's what the files are for," she said.

The blue metal box was still sitting on the table. Jenny opened it and flipped the index cards back and forth. Each card had the name of a Pets, Inc., client entered on it. There was also important information, such as the animals' feeding times and habits, and special instructions for the girls. Using the filing system, any one of them could handle any of the clients. All the information was right there in the box.

"I wrote up a card for the people who called before," Jenny went on. "They need someone to go over tomorrow and feed their ferrets."

"Ferrets?" Tina repeated.

Carrie crunched a piece of pie crust. "They're like minks—"

"Or weasels," Hilary added.

Jenny nodded. "So, who can go? Hilary?"

"Uh-uh." Hilary tugged at the horse charm she wore around her neck. "I have a horse show all day."

"We're going to Grammy Sawyer's tomorrow," Carrie reminded her sister.

Everyone looked at Tina. "I'll do it," she agreed. "Small animals are my favorites."

"Good. These are the instructions," Jenny said.

Tina took the index card and read out loud:

"Mrs. Hargett—Wesley Apartments, number Seven G. Key on ledge above door. Feed ferrets one can of cat food in morning. Refill water dish. Empty litter box and refill from bag in kitchen closet. Check around apartment for hidden food!"

"That sounds pretty simple," Carrie said.

Tina smiled. "Sure does." She slipped the card back into the filing box and shut the lid. "No problem."

# 3

"No Pets Allowed." Tina read the sign on the front door again. She swallowed hard and looked up at the big brass letters on the front of the apartment building.

"Wesley Apartments," she whispered to herself. "This is it, all right." She was positive there wasn't another Wesley Apartments in Indian Springs.

Taking a deep breath, she pulled open the front door and hurried to the elevator. The moment the elevator doors opened, she darted inside and jabbed at the seventh floor button. The elevator whooshed upward. Tina's stomach felt as if it were floating.

The elevator stopped, and the doors slid open. Tina leaned out and looked down the hallway. It was empty. Each door was painted a different color. Faint music came from behind one. A newspaper sat on the mat in front of another. Tina read their numbers: 7A, 7B, 7C . . .

The elevator doors started to close.

"Yii!" Tina yelped and leapt out into the corridor. She

darted down the empty hall toward 7G. It seemed so far away. What if someone came out and guessed why she was there? It was a no-pets building after all. By the time she got to the right door, she could hear her heart thumping. She looked around again. Of course, no one was there.

"You are such a wimp," she scolded herself. She could be visiting apartment 7G for a hundred reasons. No one would know just by looking at her that she was a pet-sitter. She faced the green-painted door, bravely. The instructions had said a key was on the upper ledge of the door frame. Tina looked up. Sure enough, she could see just the tiniest corner of a key up there. Way up there—farther than Tina could ever reach, even on tippy-tiptoes.

Tina had come this far. She couldn't leave now. If she did, those poor ferrets would go hungry, and she wouldn't deserve to be a member of Pets, Inc. What would Carrie do? she wondered. She would probably march up to one of the other doors in the hallway and ask for help. Ugh. Tina couldn't imagine doing that.

But Tina was going to get into that apartment somehow. She just had to. She took a deep breath, bent her knees, and jumped. Her fingertips brushed the ledge, but she missed the key. On the way down her knee bumped the door. The hollow *thump* echoed in the empty hallway.

Tina looked around nervously, but none of the doors opened. No one came to chase her away.

"Okay," she muttered to herself. "I can do this."

Tina made another leap at the ledge. This time her fingers brushed against the key. It fell to the floor with a musical clink. She sighed with relief and unlocked the door.

As Tina stepped inside the apartment, she heard a scuffling, scurrying sound.

"Hello?" she called. No answer.

"Come on out," she crooned. "Are you hungry?"

The scuffling sound came again from the next room. Tina walked softly to the living room. A thin, yellowish light came in through the curtains, but most of the room was in shadows. Tina squinted. "Come on out. Breakfast time!"

A dark streak scampered past her. Tina whirled around just as another streak flitted by. Two bushy brown tails flicked through the open door to the hallway and disappeared.

"Oh, no," Tina groaned.

The ferrets were loose in the hallway. And they weren't even supposed to be in the building! Tina dashed after them. She looked to her right and then to the left, but the hall was empty, and all the colored doors were shut.

"What am I going to *do?*" Tina whispered. She felt like crying. Carrie, Jenny, and Hilary were all depending on her. If she lost the Hargetts' ferrets, all of Pets, Inc., would be in trouble! Tina took a deep breath. One way or another she was going to find the ferrets and bring them home.

A rustling sound caught Tina's ear. She spun around, eyes wide. The Sunday comics were shuffling down the hall.

Tina raced after the moving newspaper. She quickly slapped her hands down on each side of the bulge underneath.

"Got you!" she cried. The lump twisted around, nosing for a way out. But Tina bundled it in her arms. Then she dashed back into apartment 7G and bumped the door shut behind her.

There was a closet to her left. Tina put the bundle of wiggly newspaper inside and shut the door firmly.

One down, one to go. She hurried back into the hall.

"If I were a ferret, where would I go?" Tina wondered out loud. She looked up and down the hallway. She couldn't see anything. Where *would* a ferret go?

At the far end of the corridor, a heavy metal door stood slightly open. It was a utility room. Inside were a sink, a stepladder, a metal cabinet, some cleaning supplies, and an open garbage chute.

Tina forced herself to cross the room and peer into the dark opening.

"Hello?" she whispered. Cool, smelly air hit her face. "Anybody there?"

Complete silence. The chute was very dark, and very, very deep. If the ferret had fallen down there, he was gone forever. Tina straightened up and leaned against the wall. She shut her eyes tight.

When Tina opened them again, she took one last hopeful glance around the room. Suddenly, a movement on top of the metal cabinet caught her attention.

"Oh!" she gasped. She blinked.

A pair of dark, gleaming brown eyes blinked back at her.

By standing on her tiptoes, Tina could see the animal on the cabinet. It did look kind of like a weasel, but it was almost as big as a small cat. It had soft beige fur and a raccoonlike black mask across its eyes.

For a moment, the two of them stared at each other. Tina was amazed at how pretty the ferret was. Its fur was shiny and silky-looking.

The ferret's nose quivered.

"Okay. Now, you're coming with me," Tina said in a firm voice. She dragged a stepladder over and climbed up. She slowly held out her hands. "Come on," she coaxed.

The ferret gave her an alert, curious look. Then he sniffed her fingers.

Tina held her breath and moved her hands carefully toward him. At last her fingers curled around the scruff of his neck. She slowly pulled him down and hugged him to her chest. His fur was even softer than she expected.

"I'm Tina," she told him. "Boy, am I glad to see you."

Moments later, she was back in the apartment with the door firmly shut.

In the kitchen, both ferrets stood on their hind legs, eagerly watching Tina open a can of cat food.

While they gobbled their breakfast, Tina sat down at the kitchen table. At last she could relax. She leaned back and rested her arm on the table. Then she noticed a piece of paper lying there—a note. She picked it up and read it. It said, "Please keep the apartment door shut at all times. Mrs. Hargett."

"Now you tell me!" Tina groaned.

The only thing left to do was empty the litter box and make a quick search for hidden food. Part of the message that made Mrs. Sawyer burn the pie crust was that the ferrets liked to hide tidbits of food around the apartment. Tina looked under the living room furniture, felt behind cushions, and checked under the beds. The ferrets followed her every step of the way. But her search turned up nothing.

Tina kneeled on the living room floor. The ferrets frisked around her, stopping every so often to sniff her legs or her hands.

24

"You guys sure are nosy," Tina giggled.

She studied them for a moment. Drawing them wouldn't be easy, she decided. They were so graceful, quick, and playful. She didn't know if she could get that in a drawing. But she would like to try. Next to pet-sitting, drawing was her favorite hobby.

"Okay. I'm leaving now," she announced firmly, then stood up. "You *stay*."

They stared back at her for a moment. Then they whisked around the corner into the kitchen. Tina opened the door and slipped out, shutting it behind her as fast as she could.

When Tina got home, her mother was sitting on the couch reading the paper. Tina collapsed next to her. "You would not believe what I just went through," she said.

Mrs. Martell looked up. "A problem?" she asked.

"Well . . . almost," Tina admitted. She told her mother the whole story. "Sometimes I don't think I belong in this business," she finished. "I'm just not naturally good at it the way Carrie is."

Mrs. Martell lowered the newspaper. "Don't be silly, honey. You handled the problem perfectly!"

"You think so?" Tina asked.

"You know you did, miss," her mother said firmly. "Carrie Sawyer couldn't have done a better job."

Tina leaned back and stretched out her legs. Maybe her mother was right. After all, she had found the ferrets and brought them back. She turned to her mother and smiled. "I definitely have to put this one in the file box," she said.

"I'll say," Mrs. Martell agreed with a chuckle.

Tina was halfway down the hall to her room when she

remembered that she didn't have the blue metal box with the file cards. It was still at the Sawyers' house. The girls were supposed to take turns keeping the box so they could all update it. But there was no way Tina could get to it now, since Carrie and Jenny were at their grandmother's.

Tina went into her room. Her black-and-white cat, Panda, was curled up on the bed. Tina picked up the bag of M&M's she had won from Carrie and flopped down next to the cat.

"We really do need a secretary," she said to Panda. "Somebody to help us organize stuff." Panda just yawned and stretched. It would be great if we had someone to answer all our phone calls so we don't get in trouble," she told the cat.

Mrs. Sawyer wasn't the only mother who was getting fed up with the phone calls. Tina's mom was an artist, and she also worked at home. She had told Tina that she was too busy to answer phone calls for the girls. Hilary's mom felt the same way. It seemed like the more business Pets, Inc., got, the more annoyed the girls' mothers became.

Tina shook out some M&M's and popped them into her mouth. One thing was for sure. If Pets, Inc., kept going this way, they'd have to go out of business. And the champion ferret trapper didn't have the slightest idea how to solve that problem.

# 4

At the end of school on Monday, Tina and Carrie raced out to get their bikes. There was a crowd in the hall. Tina slipped through it easily. Carrie took longer.

"I got creamed again," Carrie announced grimly when she got outside. Her braid was coming undone, as usual. She always seemed to get ambushed coming through the crowd.

Tina smiled as she pulled her bike out of the rack. She secretly thought Carrie always exaggerated how bad it was.

"What time are we supposed to walk Thor?" Tina asked as she hopped onto her bike.

Carrie screwed up her face. "Mrs. Murphy said four-thirty. I can't believe what a mess-up that whole thing was."

Mrs. Murphy had been one of their first customers. Pets, Inc., usually walked her Saint Bernard a couple of times a week. Thor was so gigantic, it took two girls to handle him. Mrs. Murphy had called Hilary's house while Hilary was at the horse show. Hilary already had a Monday after-school

27

job with Jenny, but her mother didn't know that. So Mrs. Burr had told Mrs. Murphy that Hilary and Jenny would walk Thor after school. The result was, Carrie and Tina had to walk Thor Monday after they went to Mrs. Archer's.

"Well," Tina said more confidently than she felt, "that means we absolutely have to leave Mrs. Archer's on time today."

"I know," Carrie agreed as they headed down the street. "She said she wants us to help move some stuff for the Firemen's Auction or something. I hope it's not just an excuse to get us to stay forever."

Tina didn't want to think about Mrs. Archer yet.

"Do you like Mr. Clark?" Tina asked Carrie to change the subject. They stopped at the corner and waited for the green light.

"The music teacher?" Carrie sucked her lower lip in and made a funny face. "He's okay."

Tina thought he was more than okay. For the whole school year, she had been thinking about how much her mother would like him. She wished somehow she could arrange for Mr. Clark and her mother to meet. Tina's father had died when she was five. Since then, Mrs. Martell had almost never gone out. Sometimes Mrs. Archer made Tina think of her mother, because without Tina, Mrs. Martell would be all alone, too.

"Why?" Carrie asked. "What about Mr. Clark?" She was riding no-handed, and waving her arms up and down like wings.

"I was just asking." She wasn't ready to tell Carrie the reason just yet.

They turned down Mrs. Archer's street and rode up her long driveway.

"Hi, girls!" Mrs. Archer pulled the door open. She was smiling as she hopped backward on her crutches. "I've been waiting for you. Come on in."

Napoleon and Josephine came trotting into the hall. Both of them wagged their tails so hard their whole bodies wobbled.

"I'm so glad you could come today," Mrs. Archer said. "I really need your help. But come into the kitchen first. You kids must be starved."

Mrs. Archer led the way. Tina and Carrie glanced at each other. They both shrugged. At least there was plenty of time until they had to leave to walk Thor.

"Now, I know I've got some pound cake here," Mrs. Archer said. "How does that sound? With a little chocolate sauce? And a glass of milk?"

"Mm-hmm!" Carrie said.

"Yes, please!" Tina cried. "Thank you."

They followed Mrs. Archer into the kitchen and sat at the table. Josie and Polie took turns drinking from the same water dish. In the corner, the lovebirds cooed in their cage.

"Now where is that chocolate sauce?" Mrs. Archer said to herself. She hobbled to the refrigerator and opened it. "Did you girls know that I grew up on a farm just outside town? We had all kinds of animals. Cows, horses—"

"Sheep?" Tina put in. She loved sheep. They were so gentle.

Mrs. Archer nodded. "A few sheep. And of course we always had *lots* of dogs. I've had dogs all my life."

Mrs. Archer took out a jar of chocolate sauce and then

set down two plates of pound cake and two glasses of milk in front of Tina and Carrie. She had a dreamy look on her face. "Every morning it was my job to collect eggs. And that one hen—what a sneak!"

"What did she do?" Carrie mumbled. Her mouth was full of cake.

"She hid her eggs in a different place every day," Mrs. Archer chuckled. "I had the devil of a time finding them, I tell you!"

Tina licked chocolate sauce off her fork and smiled. She could imagine Mrs. Archer as a girl her own age. Tina pictured her in a long skirt, searching through a hayloft for eggs. It must be a nice memory to have, she thought.

While Tina and Carrie had their cake and milk, Mrs. Archer talked on and on about her childhood on the farm.

Tina was careful to keep an eye on the clock. The minutes were ticking by. It was getting close to four. If they were going to help Mrs. Archer, they had to get started right away.

Tina nudged Carrie under the table. Mrs. Archer got up to put the teakettle on.

"We have to go soon," Tina mouthed to Carrie. She didn't want Mrs. Archer to hear.

Carrie looked puzzled.

"We have to go!" Tina moved her lips to make the words one by one. Then she jerked her head toward the clock.

"Oh!" Carrie said, forgetting to whisper.

"What's that?" Mrs. Archer asked. She turned around again and gave them both a curious smile.

Carrie looked down at the table.

Tina sat up as straight as she could. "We have to go pretty soon," she explained. "We have another job."

Mrs. Archer's smile disappeared. "Oh, dear. I was hoping you girls could help me bring some things downstairs for the Firemen's Auction.

The kettle started to whistle, and Mrs. Archer turned back to the stove. "I didn't realize you girls had such a tight schedule," she said quietly.

Tina felt awful. She was pretty sure she had hurt Mrs. Archer's feelings. She met Carrie's eyes and turned up both of her hands.

"One of us will have to stay," Carrie whispered into Tina's ear. "We said we'd help."

That meant only one of them would walk Thor. Tina's stomach did a flip-flop.

"I'll go walk Thor," she said, forcing herself to sound positive.

"Are you sure?" Carrie whispered.

Tina nodded. "I'll do it. I really don't mind," she said.

But she wasn't sure at all. She was a little bit afraid of Thor, even though she knew that was babyish of her. Carrie wasn't the least bit afraid of him.

"Well . . ." Carrie twirled her empty glass around. "Is that okay, Mrs. Archer?" she asked.

Mrs. Archer was dunking a teabag in a steaming mug. She looked over her shoulder. "What's that, dear?"

"I can stay and help you, but Tina has to go walk somebody's dog," Carrie explained.

Mrs. Archer nodded and went back to making her tea.

Tina and Carrie glanced at each other. They couldn't help

feeling as if they were letting Mrs. Archer down. But Pets, Inc., had a responsibility to Mrs. Murphy, too.

When Tina got to Mrs. Murphy's house, she stood up as straight as she could and rang the doorbell.

"Hi, Tina," Mrs. Murphy said, opening the door wide. She looked past Tina to the street. She seemed a little surprised. Behind her, Thor was standing still and panting. "Did you come alone?"

Tina swallowed hard. "Hi, Mrs. Murphy. Yes, I did. But don't worry. I can do it."

"I'm sure you can," the woman said. She handed Thor's leash to Tina. "He looks intimidating, but he's a big puppy at heart. A nice long walk now. He needs some exercise."

Tina swallowed. The first time Pets, Inc., had met Thor, it had taken all four of them to budge him. He was huge.

But Tina didn't want Mrs. Murphy to realize that she was nervous about him. She didn't want Thor to realize it, either. So she put on a smile and led Thor down the front steps. Then she turned and waved to Mrs. Murphy.

Thor walked to the end of the driveway. There he stopped and studied the possibilities in both directions. "Okay. Come on, boy." Tina tugged at Thor's leash. Thor didn't move.

Mrs. Murphy was still watching from the door.

Tina kept her smile in place. She tugged on Thor's leash again. "Come on, Thor. Let's go."

While Tina pulled on the leash, Thor looked up and down the street. Then he started moving. The leash almost yanked Tina off her feet, but she hurried along behind him.

"Whoa, boy," she cried. She almost had to run to keep up. "Slow down."

But Thor's pace just picked up even more. He seemed to have found a good scent to follow. His huge tail wagged back and forth as he raced ahead.

Tina's feet went slapping along the sidewalk. She was half-walking, half-running. She tried to slow down, but Thor didn't notice, or else he didn't care.

At the corner of Jefferson Street, the girls usually turned right with Thor. But today Thor had a different idea. Without pausing, he followed the curve of the sidewalk on around to the left.

Tina was starting to pant. Her hand hurt where she was holding on to the leash. *She* was the one being walked, not Thor. He was deciding where to go and how fast to go there. Tina felt like a balloon at the end of a string.

"Thor, slow down," she huffed. She looked around. She hoped no one was watching them. She probably looked pretty silly.

*He's never going to stop,* Tina told herself. *He'll just keep going and going and going. We'll wind up in Florida. Or maybe California.* Tina wasn't even sure which way they were going anymore. Keeping up took all her attention. It really wasn't very funny, after all. Tears started to well up in her eyes.

*Don't cry,* she told herself. *Don't cry!*

A man in a car slowed down and stared as he passed. Two kids across the street watched as the huge dog towed her along.

Then Thor spotted a squirrel and started to run.

Tina shot forward. "Ow!" she cried. That was it! Now she was mad. She grabbed the leash with both hands and yanked back on it.

"NO! THOR! STAY!" she yelled as loud as she could.

Thor stopped. He looked back at her, panting.

Tina was panting, too. She stared at the dog. He was waiting patiently for her next command. For a moment, Tina was too surprised to say anything. She couldn't believe she had really stopped him.

Finally, she let out a heavy sigh. "Good boy," she said. She petted his head cautiously. He panted.

Tina looked down at him. His huge brown eyes had droopy lids. His lips were droopy, too. His long tongue hung out of one side of his mouth.

Tina began to giggle. He looked so funny. How could she have been afraid of such a goofy-looking dog? He was big and not too well behaved, but he was really very gentle, just as Mrs. Murphy had said.

Tina squatted in front of Thor and looked into his eyes. "You're not so bad, are you?"

Thor panted. Then his long, drippy tongue slurped across her cheek.

Tina scrunched up her mouth. "Yuck."

She wiped her cheek off with her sleeve and stood up. It was a sloppy, slurpy kiss, but it was still a kiss. Thor liked her. Tina smiled at him and scratched his chest with one finger.

"Okay," she said firmly. "Let's go. *Slowly.*"

Tina kept expecting Thor to start racing ahead again. But to her relief, he walked peacefully at her side. Now that he knew she was the boss, he let her take charge.

"He was just fine," she told Mrs. Murphy when she

brought him back. She handed over the leash and tried not to look too glad the job was over.

"Well, I knew he wouldn't be any trouble," Mrs. Murphy said. She unclipped the leash. "He's a good boy."

Tina nodded, rubbing her sore shoulder. "He is," she said truthfully.

What would she have done if he hadn't been a good boy? Tina wondered. She was still surprised and happy that she'd been able to control him. One skinny fourth-grader with a giant dog like Thor was not a very good combination. This time everything had turned out okay, but it could have been a disaster. The job would have been much easier if Carrie had been with her.

But Carrie had had to stay at Mrs. Archer's.

That thought reminded Tina of another problem of Pets, Inc.—a problem she still didn't know how to solve.

More and more, it seemed, helping Mrs. Archer was hurting Pets, Inc.

# 5

"You know what my mom said to me yesterday?" Tina asked Carrie.

They were riding to Mrs. Archer's. It was the corgis' usual Saturday morning bathtime.

"She said I get more phone calls than she does." Tina looked down at her feet. She was wearing her white sneakers that she had drawn designs all over. She watched a tic-tac-toe symbol go around and around as she pedaled.

"She said every time she sits down to start working, somebody calls," Tina went on. She imitated her mother's voice. " 'Another hungry turtle, Tina.' At first she was proud we were getting so much business. But I can tell she doesn't think it's so great anymore."

Carrie didn't say anything.

Tina knew the number of phone calls to the Sawyers were getting pretty large, too. And Mrs. Sawyer depended on her phone for her own business.

"Has your mom mentioned it, too?" Tina asked nervously.

Carrie didn't answer, but she rolled her eyes and let out a big sigh. "I just want to do all the jobs I have to do this weekend. That's all I want to think about."

For the rest of the ride to Mrs. Archer's, Tina was deep in thought. Their pet business was going well, but it was in big trouble at the same time. If their mothers got really fed up with all the phone calls, what would Pets, Inc., do? They didn't have any other way to get business. It was really beginning to worry Tina.

Carrie rang Mrs. Archer's doorbell. Tina took a deep breath and let it out slowly.

"Surprise!" Mrs. Archer threw the door open and beamed at them. Napoleon and Josephine were right behind her, noses twitching.

Tina and Carrie stared.

"You aren't using your crutches!" Carrie gasped.

Mrs. Archer waved the wooden cane she was holding. "That's right. I just need this for a little while now. Isn't it just grand?" She lifted her chin and struck a dramatic prose.

Tina couldn't help laughing. "That's really great. I bet you feel a lot better."

"I certainly do," said Mrs. Archer. She stepped back and flung out one hand. "After you, ladies."

Tina and Carrie giggled as they went into the hall. The corgis seemed to know that everyone was happy. Josie let out a yip, and Polie danced around in a small circle.

"Now, into the tub, into the tub," Mrs. Archer said. She shooed the dogs ahead of her. "I'm just baking up a batch of my famous chocolate surprise cookies," she added.

Tina suddenly felt so happy that she couldn't stop smiling. She was so used to seeing Mrs. Archer on crutches, she had nearly forgotten that one day she wouldn't need them anymore. Now Mrs. Archer's problems and theirs were all solved.

"I'm glad she can walk now, aren't you?" Tina whispered to Carrie.

Carrie nodded, turning on the faucets. "Maybe now she can go visiting her friends and stuff."

"Boy," Tina sighed. "I'd hate to be on crutches for so long."

"Not me!" Carrie stood on one foot and tried hopping around. The dogs bustled along beside her. "I wish I could have crutches for a while. I bet it would be fun."

Tina wrinkled her nose. "You wouldn't be able to ride your bike, you know." Carrie wasn't paying any attention to filling the tub. Tina put a finger in the water to test the temperature. It was just right. She scooped up Josie. "Come on. Let's hurry up," she said to the dog.

Josie looked up at her with a pathetic expression. "Chicken," Tina murmured. She studied the look in Josie's eyes, trying to memorize it in case she needed to draw it one day. Then she firmly put the dog into the warm, soapy water.

Tina and Carrie washed the dogs and dried them. When Tina pulled the plug in the bathtub, she and Carrie carefully watched the water go down. They were looking to see if any fleas had been rinsed out of the dogs' fur.

"I guess they're clean," Tina announced, as the last of the water whirled down the drain.

Carrie stood up. She had a hair in her mouth that she kept trying to grab. It didn't look like she was getting it, though.

"Yuck. Thoap on my tongue," she lisped. She made a face.

Tina grinned. "Let's go see if Mrs. Archer's finished her cookies."

After the girls had each eaten a handful of Mrs. Archer's cookies, Carrie cleaned and disinfected the lovebirds' cage while Mrs. Archer and Tina held the birds.

"I remember when I was your age," Mrs. Archer said. Her eyes had a distant look. "Indian Springs was a very different town then, you know."

"How?" Carrie asked.

As Mrs. Archer answered, Tina carefully loosened her grip on the bird. Her fingers made a strong but gentle cage. She could feel the bird's heart beating through the silky, delicate feathers. Very slowly, she lifted the lovebird. The bird blinked and tipped his head sideways.

"And then, of course, when my children were young, this house was crowded day and night," Mrs. Archer was saying. "Oh, it keeps you young to have kids around." She sighed. She gave both girls a fond smile.

Tina glanced over at Carrie. There was a short silence.

"Cage is all finished," Carrie announced. She wiped the wire bars one more time with a paper towel.

Tina stood up and put the bird back in. Then she stood back so Mrs. Archer could put the other one in.

"Well," Carrie said. "I guess we should go."

Tina nodded. They were finished. There was no reason not to go. But somehow Tina felt guilty, as though they were abandoning poor Mrs. Archer. She could tell Carrie felt the same way.

"I won't hold you up," Mrs. Archer said. She took her

pocketbook from the kitchen counter. Then she took off her regular glasses and put on her reading glasses. She counted out three dollars for each of them. "You're both good girls. Thank you."

The girls made a stop around the corner to feed the Mortons' hamsters. Then they rode to Carrie's house for lunch. After they had eaten, they went upstairs to Carrie's room.

Carrie was trying to get Caledonia to be friends with Feather, her parakeet. First, she had brought Caledonia into the room to look at Feather in his cage. Then, she had carefully held Feather and let Caledonia look at the bird from a short distance. Now, Carrie was sitting on her bed. Feather was perched on Carrie's arm while Caledonia nestled at her feet. Tina stared at the three of them through the wrong end of some binoculars. They appeared faraway and tiny.

Caledonia kept leaping up, lunging toward the parakeet. Each time, Feather would scurry up Carrie's arm to her shoulder. Then the little parakeet would slowly walk back down again.

"Caledonia's going to bite Feather's head right off," Tina warned.

"No, she won't." Carrie sounded very sure. "Caledonia, be nice," she warned. She tapped the puppy's nose. "*No.*"

Caledonia sat back on the bed. She cocked her head and looked at Feather.

"You know what I was thinking?" Tina turned the binoculars around the right way. Now she had a close-up view of Caledonia's floppy ears. She could see all the individual hairs. At a normal distance, they looked shiny brown. But they were really a mixture of shades, from dark brown to white.

"What?" Carrie asked.

Tina turned the binoculars on Carrie. "Well . . ." She cleared her throat. "Do you think it would be a good idea if we all went over to Mrs. Archer's tomorrow? To say good-bye and thanks for being a good customer?"

"You mean, since she can walk now?" Carrie asked.

"Right," Tina said. "She's been so nice to us. Giving us cookies all the time."

"That's a good idea, Tina," Carrie said. She let Feather hop from her left index finger to her right index finger and back again. "I'll ask Jenny, and she can call Hilary," Carrie added.

"Good." Tina finally lowered the binoculars.

"It'll be good to say good-bye to Mrs. Archer, but I—" Carrie stopped in midsentence when the telephone rang. Both of them listened. Carrie looked as if she were ready to jump up.

But the phone rang only once. Carrie turned back to her animals.

"Carrie!" Mrs. Sawyer called up the stairs.

"I'm coming, Mom!" Carrie called. She leapt up and ran for the door. Feather took off and fluttered to the curtain rod. Caledonia raced after Carrie.

When Carrie and Caledonia were gone, the room seemed very quiet. Tina listened to hear if the call was for Pets, Inc.

There had been two calls for Pets, Inc., during lunch. Then Carrie's father, who was a lawyer, had said he was going to his office for some peace and quiet.

Tina heard muffled voices on the stairs. It was Carrie and Mrs. Sawyer. Tina couldn't hear the words, but she could tell they were arguing. A few moments later, Carrie came back.

"It was just Mrs. Morton calling to say thanks," Carrie explained.

"Oh," Tina said. "That was nice of her."

Carrie nodded. "We have to go downstairs now," she muttered. Her face was pink. "To the kitchen."

Tina gulped and looked away. She hated to hear her friend being scolded. "Okay," she said.

"We have to go to the kitchen so I can answer the phone," Carrie explained.

Tina nodded. "Okay." She followed Carrie into the hall.

"It's not fair," Carrie said. Her chin was quivering. "How else can we get jobs?"

Tina shrugged. She felt sorry and nervous at the same time. "I don't know," she whispered.

Carrie and Tina sat down together at the kitchen table. The oven timer tick-ticked in the silence. There was a cake baking. It smelled delicious. Tina guessed it was for Mrs. Sawyer's catering business.

"Want to play cards or something?" Carrie asked. She still looked a little upset.

"Okay," Tina agreed quickly.

Carrie scraped her chair back. "I'll just go get some cards. I'll be right back." Her footsteps plodded down the hall.

Tina slumped in her chair. She felt terrible.

A moment later, the telephone rang. Tina froze.

"I'll get it!" Carrie shrieked. She slammed the door open

and came racing through the kitchen. She grabbed the receiver. "Hello?"

Tina bit her lip and watched her best friend.

"Okay, sure," Carrie said into the phone. She wrote something down on a pad. "Okay. Yes. Thank you. Bye."

When Carrie hung up the phone, she sat down again at the table. She tried to look optimistic. "Another job."

"That's good," Tina replied.

The kitchen door swung open, and Mrs. Sawyer came in. Tina felt her cheeks burn. Carrie had answered her own call, but Mrs. Sawyer still looked unhappy.

"Carrie, did I hear you running?" The way she said it, Tina knew it was one of those questions grown-ups ask even though they already know the answer perfectly well.

Carrie's face went pink. "Ummm . . ."

"You know this angel food cake is very delicate," her mother went on. "Vibrations could make it fall . . ."

She switched on the oven light and peered in through the window. There was a tense silence.

Tina stared across the table at Carrie. Her friend looked frightened.

"Is it okay, Mom?" Carrie squeaked.

Mrs. Sawyer let out a long breath. She switched off the oven light, switched off the oven, and shook her head.

"There's nothing I can do about it now," she said in a tired voice. She looked sadly at Carrie and Tina and left the room.

"Is it ruined?" Tina whispered. Her mouth felt dry.

Without answering, Carrie got up, switched on the oven light, and looked in. Then she burst into tears. Tina knew exactly how she felt.

# 6

The group planned to meet at Fountain Park on Sunday morning. Tina was the first one to arrive. The park was a good meeting point for all of them.

"Hey! Tina!"

Tina looked up. Carrie and Jenny were riding toward her. Carrie was waving both arms in the air.

"Hi, you guys," Tina said when they came closer.

Carrie stopped beside a statue. She stuck out one leg and propped herself up against it.

Tina pulled her bike up next to Carrie's. Something on the ground caught her eye. She looked more closely. It was a duck feather. Tina bent down to pick it up. She examined its thin shaft and the way the feathers moved when she ran her fingers across them, first one direction then the other.

Jenny frowned at her wristwatch. "Hilary's late."

"No, she's not," Carrie said. "Here she comes."

Hilary coasted down the short hill toward them. She was wearing old jeans and lace-up boots with rubbers over them.

Tina knew that was what Hilary always wore when she was mucking out horse stalls in her family's stable.

"I had to do stalls this morning," Hilary explained, hopping off next to the statue. Some dirt and sawdust clung to Hilary's heel. She scraped her foot across the grass until it was all gone.

"Well . . ." Jenny looked at everyone. "Let's go."

They all pushed off. Tina rode next to Carrie, and Hilary rode next to Jenny.

"Want to sing something?" Hilary called out. She looked back at Tina and Carrie. She liked to sing, and had a pretty good voice.

Carrie shrugged. "Like what?"

"I know," Tina piped up. She liked singing, too, even though she couldn't sing as well as Hilary. "How about this one?" She asked, and began to hum a song Mr. Clark had taught them in music class just a week before.

Hilary's face lit up. "Yeah! 'Will the Circle Be Unbroken?' That's a good one. Mr. Clark taught us that last year, too."

Hilary started the song. Tina followed along, smiling to herself. She liked the happy, hopeful sound of the song. And she liked the way Mr. Clark sang it to them. He sounded like a real singer on a record.

Carrie was belting out the words. Tina winced. Carrie was out of tune. Tina pedaled quickly, to catch up with Hilary and Jenny.

As she rode alongside the two older girls, Tina was thinking about how much she liked Mr. Clark, and wondering if there was any way to introduce him to her mother. If she did really bad work in music class, Mr. Clark would have to talk to her mother. Maybe that wasn't such a good idea, though. Tina didn't want to get in trouble on purpose.

But there had to be a way she could introduce her mother to Mr. Clark. Her mother liked to sing, too.

"I'm kind of sad we won't be working for Mrs. Archer anymore, aren't you?"

Tina blinked. She realized Carrie was talking to her. They all pulled up at the end of Mrs. Archer's driveway. It was the last time they would ride up to the big brick house.

"Yeah, I am," she agreed softly.

"She's really nice," Hilary put in. "But every time I ever went there, she made me so late."

Jenny nodded. "I guess it's really better this way." She made a face. "I mean, we have so many other clients, right?"

The others looked at Jenny, and then looked away. Tina felt a little bit lonely. "Yeah," she said in a quiet voice.

Jenny began squeezing her brake handles and letting them go. "Well . . ." Her voice trailed off.

Carrie kicked off and rode up the driveway. "Come on," she called.

Nobody looked at anybody else as they went up to the door. Nobody said anything, either. Tina edged behind Carrie. She knew it had been her idea to go. But now she wished she hadn't ever thought of it.

"Well! Hello!" Mrs. Archer said, opening the door. The corgis peeked out from behind her. "And to what do I owe this nice surprise?"

For a moment, no one spoke. Tina didn't want to be the first one to say it. She looked at Napoleon and Josephine. They looked as happy and friendly as ever.

"Well," Carrie began. She looked around at the others.

47

"We wanted to just come over and say we really liked working for you. We wanted to thank you for all the cookies and stuff you always gave us."

Mrs. Archer looked perplexed. She was still smiling, but her forehead was wrinkled with tiny lines. "I'm sorry," she said. "I don't. . . ?" She stopped and looked at Jenny.

"We wanted to say good-bye, since you don't need us anymore," Jenny explained.

"Don't—but I do!" Mrs. Archer gasped. "I haven't asked you to stop!"

"No?" Carrie whispered.

Mrs. Archer shook her head and laughed. "No!"

"Oh, I—we thought," Jenny stammered.

"No, not at all." Mrs. Archer shook her head and let out a warm chuckle. "I don't know how I'd manage without you girls helping me. But it was a very sweet thought. Come on in."

Without a word, the four members of Pets, Inc., trooped into the hallway.

"Let me see if I can find you girls some fudge," Mrs. Archer said.

Tina plucked at the back of Carrie's T-shirt. "Now what?" she whispered while the others went on ahead.

"I don't know," Carrie hissed back. There was nothing to do but go in.

They all sat around Mrs. Archer's kitchen table. It was a familiar place to all of them now. It felt as if they'd been visiting Mrs. Archer for years—sitting around her kitchen table and eating snacks. How would they ever explain to her why they couldn't keep coming?

Tina couldn't meet anybody's eyes. Hilary slid her horse

pendant quickly back and forth. Meanwhile, Jenny kept fidgeting. One minute she was sitting up very straight, the next she was leaning back, staring at the ceiling. Tina couldn't remember ever seeing Jenny Sawyer so nervous before.

"My, you girls are awfully quiet this morning," Mrs. Archer teased. She stopped bustling around and looked at them all. "Is something wrong?"

"No!" Carrie squeaked. She looked at Tina and gulped.

Tina wanted to run away.

"Well, now. What was it I wanted to show Hilary?" Mrs. Archer went on. "Of course! I'll be right back." Mrs. Archer left the kitchen.

Tina nibbled at a corner of her fudge and put it back on the table. Everyone was being so quiet, Tina held her breath.

Finally, Hilary broke the silence. "I feel so stupid!" she whispered loudly.

"Me, too!" agreed Jenny. "I don't know what to say."

"We agreed," Jenny went on in a low voice. "We agreed we have too many clients. She takes up more time than anyone."

"I know," Carrie put in, taking a huge bite of her fudge. Tina didn't know how Carrie could eat anything. "But we can't say that to her!"

Hilary let go of her horse pendant. "There's no way we can get out of it, is there?" she asked in a strangled voice. "Couldn't we just say we're quitting the whole thing? Ending Pets, Inc.?"

"Oh, come on!" Carrie let out a funny snorting sound. "We can't tell her that!" she said loudly.

"Well, who's going to tell her she makes us late all the time?" Hilary shot back.

Tina glanced quickly at the door. Her throat felt tight and dry. She didn't think she'd be able to say anything, even if she wanted to. This was the first real argument they ever had about Pets, Inc. She stared at the piece of fudge in front of her and wondered if she'd ever be able to eat fudge again.

"It probably doesn't even matter anymore," Jenny said. "We might have to quit working anyway. Mom said she's had it up to here with the phone calls." Jenny made a slice across her throat with one hand.

"My mom, too," Hilary put in.

"Hardly anybody calls you," Carrie said angrily. "Most people call our house."

"That's not true!"

Tina caught her breath. "You guys!" she gasped. "Shh!"

"Well, it's true," Jenny went on in a whisper. "If we can't figure out what to do about the phone, we might have to quit. So it doesn't even matter anymore if Mrs. Archer is spoiling our business."

The door opened, and they all froze. Jenny's mouth was still open. Mrs. Archer came in, holding a scrapbook.

Tina took one look at Mrs. Archer's face and knew that she'd heard everything.

"Here it is," Mrs. Archer said, laying the scrapbook on the table. Her voice was low. She didn't look at any of them. "If you're interested, you could look at it sometime."

Hilary cleared her throat. "Thanks," she said. She sounded like she was trying to stay calm. But it wasn't working.

"You know, I was thinking." Mrs. Archer turned her back

50

to them and started to fill the teakettle. "Now that I'm on my feet again, I guess I really don't need your help."

Tina pressed her knees together and made her hands into tight fists. She didn't dare look up.

"I need to be more independent, anyway," Mrs. Archer went on. "You were a great help, but I can handle the dogs now."

There was a long silence. Somebody swallowed loudly enough for everyone else to hear.

"Okay," Hilary said after a minute. Her voice was hollow.

"So." Mrs. Archer straightened her back, and faced them again. She was smiling, but she didn't look very happy. "Why don't you kids run along now? I know you probably have other pets to look after today."

Tina got out of her chair so fast, it almost tipped over. Her cheeks were burning. "Bye, Mrs. Archer," she whispered.

Without waiting to see what anyone else would do, she turned and ran from the room.

# 7

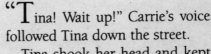

"Tina! Wait up!" Carrie's voice followed Tina down the street.

Tina shook her head and kept pedaling. She didn't want to talk to anybody, not even Carrie. She had never felt more ashamed of herself.

When she got to the park entrance, Tina veered in. She coasted down the hill to the duck pond.

"Tina!"

Tina stopped and got off her bike. Her eyes were stinging, and her nose itched. She blinked and poked one finger behind her glasses to wipe away a tear.

It was all her fault. She should have told Mrs. Archer the truth the very first time Mrs. Archer had made Carrie and her stay late. She should have said that Pets, Inc., was exactly what the name said: a business for taking care of pets. Period. Instead, they had let it get out of control, and now they had hurt someone whom they'd meant to help.

Tina's chin trembled. Everything ahead of her looked

blurry. She was always wishing she were more like Carrie. Carrie could tell anybody anything, but Tina couldn't expect Carrie to handle every situation. This time, Carrie hadn't told Mrs. Archer, either.

One by one, the others rolled to a stop beside the duck pond.

Nobody said a word.

The white ducks swam around the pond, making the soft, whistling *quack* that she usually liked listening to so much. Every once in a while, one of them would dive, tail up, with its head underwater and its orange feet splashing. Usually the girls all enjoyed watching them, but not today.

Tina looked up. It was obvious that the others felt as awful as she did. Carrie was pushing at her kickstand with one toe. Hilary was straddling her bike and looking at the ground. Jenny was gazing back the way they had come.

Sniffling, Tina opened her bike basket. There was a plastic bag of stale bread crusts inside. She took it out and silently crumbled the bread into small pieces.

"I feel like the biggest jerk in the world," Carrie muttered.

"Me, too," Hilary said.

Jenny sighed. "Me, three."

Tina had a lump in her throat and didn't trust herself to say anything. She threw a handful of crumbs into the water. The ducks swam toward her and began gobbling the bread.

"Maybe there wasn't any other way, though," Jenny added. She kicked at one of her pedals.

"At least we don't have to worry about her making us late anymore," Hilary put in.

Carrie dug the toe of her sneaker into the dirt. "Yeah."

54

Tina threw another handful of crumbs into the pond so hard the ducks were startled.

"I mean, we need all the extra time we have," Jenny said, sounding as though she didn't really believe it. "Don't we?"

Hilary shrugged. "I guess," she said.

"Right, Carrie?" Jenny said.

Carrie jutted her chin out. "Yeah," she whispered. "Right."

Tina knew Jenny would ask her next. But she couldn't look up.

There was a long silence. "Tina?" Jenny said. Tina swallowed hard a few times. The lump in her throat wouldn't go away. Finally, she raised her eyes. "Right," she said. She grabbed the last crumbs and flung them into the water.

Even though she was agreeing with her friends, she felt like a traitor.

"I have to go home now," she said. Without looking up, she got on her bike and rode away.

She was crying so hard, she could barely see. She rode as fast as she could, as though something were chasing her. For the first time, she didn't care if her friends thought she was a baby.

When her own one-story blue house came into view, Tina took a deep breath and wiped her eyes. She didn't want her mother to see how upset she was. Mrs. Martell always fussed when Tina was the tiniest bit unhappy.

Tina's mother was in her art studio with the door open. She was painting with watercolors. She wore an absorbed, studious expression. Even on Sundays, Mrs. Martell worked hard. Yin and Yang, the dogs, were stretched out on an easy chair, looking out the window. They both turned around, their tongues hanging out, when Tina poked her head in the door.

"Hi, Mom," Tina said. She kept her eyes down and her voice steady. She hoped her mother was too busy to notice anything wrong.

"Hi, Tina," Mrs. Martell called. She held out her left hand without looking away from her painting. "There's a message for you by the phone."

Tina had to swallow before she could speak. "Okay."

She was glad her voice had sounded pretty normal.

When she was out of sight, she wiped her eyes again with the back of her hand. In the kitchen, she picked up the message pad and read her mother's note.

"MRS. TENDYKE HAS A JOB FOR YOU. PLEASE COME OVER TODAY AT TWO. 16 WHITNEY COURT."

Tina walked back down the hall. "Mom?"

Her mother swirled her paintbrush in a glass of water, coloring it a beautiful blue. "Mmmm?"

Tina frowned. "Did Mrs. Tendyke say what kind of pet she has?"

"Now, let me think." Mrs. Martell tapped her chin with one long, paint-stained finger. "She said she heard about you from Mrs. Ballard."

Mrs. Ballard was one of Tina's clients. She had an overweight dachshund that Tina exercised twice a week. Her house was on Whitney Court, too.

"Anything else?" Tina asked.

"I'm sorry, Tina. I didn't ask for all the details," her mother explained. "You know what I'm like when I'm working."

Tina nodded. She just hoped it wouldn't be another

57

difficult job, like gigantic Thor or the Hargetts' escape-artist ferrets. She really could use a break.

Tina wandered back to the kitchen. Pets, Inc., really was getting more clients all the time, so it was a good thing they weren't working for Mrs. Archer anymore. Sooner or later, they would have had to let her down. Now it was done, and it was for the best, Tina told herself.

Wasn't it?

# 8

"Hi, Mrs. Tendyke. I'm Tina Martell." Tina put out her hand and smiled her friendliest smile.

Mrs. Tendyke shook Tina's hand quickly then ran her fingers through her red hair. "Oh, I'm so glad you could come." She looked frazzled. "We just moved in a few days ago. Mrs. Ballard said you're a very nice girl."

"Thank you," Tina said shyly. She followed Mrs. Tendyke inside. Then, remembering her business manners, she asked, "What kind of pet do you have?"

Mrs. Tendyke turned around. She had a surprised smile on her face. "My little girls have a rabbit," she said. "Mrs. Ballard didn't tell me you were a detective, too."

Tina smiled back politely, even though she didn't quite understand what Mrs. Tendyke meant.

"Are you going away for a few days?" Tina asked.

"Good heavens, no! Just a couple of hours," Mrs. Tendyke replied.

Tina's smile slipped. Why would Mrs. Tendyke need

someone to take care of her rabbit for just a few hours? Maybe it would all become clearer if she just waited and listened. She decided to keep quiet and pay close attention to everything Mrs. Tendyke said.

Mrs. Tendyke led Tina into the kitchen. "Apple juice in the fridge. Teddy Grahams in the cupboard over the sink. Emergency numbers by the phone."

Tina looked where Mrs. Tendyke pointed, nodding slowly. Apple juice? Cookies? Emergency numbers? For a *rabbit*? It must be a very special kind of rabbit, she thought. Tina tried to look confident.

"What grade are you in?" Mrs. Tendyke asked her.

Tina stood up straight. "Fourth," she said proudly. She hoped she sounded grown-up.

Mrs. Tendyke raised her eyebrows. "Oh. Well," she said tiredly. "Just for a couple of hours. I guess you can manage."

Something was definitely not right. Tina swallowed. She knew she had to say something. For a moment, she wiggled her toes back and forth inside her sneakers.

"Umm," she began finally. "Is there something—special about it I need to know?" She pushed up her glasses. "I mean, is it valuable, or sick, or something?"

Mrs. Tendyke was rummaging in her purse. She glanced up. "It?" she repeated. She gave Tina a strange look.

"The rabbit," Tina said.

"The rabbit? *Bugsy?*" Mrs. Tendyke laughed. She opened the back door. "Don't worry about him. He takes care of himself. Girls! Come on inside!"

Now it was Tina's turn to give Mrs. Tendyke a strange look. "Then what do you want me to do?" she asked.

"What do I—" Mrs. Tendyke broke off as two little red-haired girls came through the door. They stood on either side of their mother. Mrs. Tendyke put a hand on each of their heads. "Just normal baby-sitting," she said. "Nothing special."

Tina felt her eyes widen. She stared at the two little girls. They both smiled up at her. A warm blush ran up Tina's throat. They weren't much younger than she was. Someone had made a big mistake. She just hoped it wasn't her!

Her eyes flew up to Mrs. Tendyke again. "But—I'm not allowed to baby-sit," she whispered.

Mrs. Tendyke looked completely baffled. "But—Mrs. Ballard said you always took such good care of her little boy."

"I . . . I think maybe she meant . . . Toby," Tina said hesitantly. She licked her lips. Tina never sat for Mrs. Ballard's baby boy, Benjamin.

Mrs. Tendyke still looked confused. "But isn't Toby the name of her—"

"Dog," Tina said. She looked down at her sneakers.

"Her *dog*?" Mrs. Tendyke sounded like she didn't want to believe it.

Tina nodded. Her eyes were wide and apologetic.

"Now wait just a moment, here. I distinctly remember . . ." Mrs. Tendyke went to the telephone and picked up the pad lying beside it. "I called Mrs. Ballard and asked for numbers for a plumber, a baby-sitter, and a—"

She stopped and snapped her mouth shut. Then she looked at Tina sheepishly. "And someone good with animals." She gulped. "Are you . . . ?"

Tina nodded. "I'm sorry," she said. "I take care of Toby."

"Oh, no." Mrs. Tendyke sat down hard. Her little girls stared round-eyed at Tina. "I called the wrong person!"

Tina felt partly relieved. But she felt sorry that Mrs. Tendyke's plans were going to be ruined. She looked up at Mrs. Tendyke. Mrs. Tendyke looked as if she were feeling awfully dumb. Tina couldn't help feeling sorry for her.

"I guess you couldn't baby-sit, just this one time?" Mrs. Tendyke asked. She didn't sound very hopeful.

"I don't think so," Tina said quietly. "My mother says not until I'm twelve."

"Well, there goes that idea," Mrs. Tendyke sighed. She flipped her pencil onto the table and let her arms hang at her sides.

"I'm sorry," Tina whispered.

The woman shook her head. Bright red curls bounced around her face. "Oh, it's my fault," she said in a cheerful voice. "I should've been paying attention. Thanks for coming over, Tina."

Tina smiled back weakly. "You're welcome." She waved one hand toward the door. "I guess . . ."

"Right." Mrs. Tendyke got up and walked Tina to the door. "I'm sorry," she said, shaking Tina's hand. "And I promise I'll call you when I do need someone to take care of Bugsy."

"Well, good-bye," Tina said. She walked down the steps, climbed back on her bike, and pedaled down the block.

In the beginning, Pets, Inc., was just fun. They took care of animals. And that was all there was to it. But now it was more complicated. Tina and her friends were getting in trouble with too many phone calls. They'd hurt Mrs. Archer's feelings. Everyone worried about it all the time, just like a real business. It wasn't supposed to be that way, but it was. It was all getting to be too much for them, Tina

62

thought. Maybe they'd be better off if they just gave up. Tina swallowed. She felt disloyal even thinking such a thing. But she couldn't help it. Pets, Inc., was starting to be more trouble than it was worth.

# 9

By the time Tina got home she was worn out with worry. "Hi, Mom," she mumbled, slumping in her favorite armchair. Panda walked by. Tina scooped him up and buried her face in his warm fur.

"Hi, Tina. What's wrong?" Mrs. Martell stood in the doorway of her studio.

"That lady wanted a baby-sitter," Tina said. Panda's fur muffled her voice.

Her mother took a few steps toward Tina. "What?" she asked.

Tina sighed and let Panda slip out of her arms. She watched him walk away. "That lady wanted a baby-sitter," she repeated. She looked up at her mother. "I wish you could've asked what she wanted."

"Oh, I'm sorry, honey," Mrs. Martell replied. "I just assumed . . ."

"Yeah, but—" Tina began.

"Tina, I really am sorry." Her mother took another step

closer and reached for Tina's hand. "And I know it's hard, trying to run a business. But I have to work, too." She squeezed Tina's hand. "For both of us."

"I know, Mom," Tina whispered.

"I don't really mind the calls, Tina," her mother added. "There aren't *that* many. But you can't expect me to be your secretary when you aren't here."

The phone rang. Tina glanced up at her mother.

Mrs. Martell arched one eyebrow. "I think maybe you should answer it, Teen. It's probably for you."

It was Carrie. Tina leaned her elbows on the kitchen counter and pressed the phone against her ear with her shoulder.

"What's up?" she asked.

"You're never going to believe this," Carrie said. She sounded worried.

"What?"

There was a short pause. "Remember how I borrowed that special shedding comb from Mrs. Archer?" Carrie asked. "To use on Caledonia?"

Tina nodded. Something told her it was going to be bad news. She twirled a pencil between two fingers. "Yeah," she said slowly.

"I still have it."

Tina's eyes opened wide. The pencil bounced on the counter. "You—"

"We have to take it back, Teen."

The last thing Tina wanted to do that afternoon was to go see Mrs. Archer again. She felt bad enough already. "Why can't Jenny go with you?"

"She's not home," Carrie explained. "I think she had a job with Hilary."

"But, Carrie—"

"I'll never ask you for another favor in my whole life. I swear." Carrie sounded desperate. "We'll just put it on the back porch really quietly. She'll never even know we were there till we're gone."

"You mean, sneak up to the house?" Tina said. "I don't know . . ."

"Tina!" Carrie's voice was tearful. "Please?"

"Okay," Tina agreed in a low voice. She really didn't want to do it, but she couldn't let her best friend down.

Carrie let out a long sigh. "Thanks."

"You know," Tina added. "This is turning out to be the most horrible weekend of my life."

"Did something else happen?" Carrie asked.

Tina pictured Mrs. Tendyke's little red-haired girls staring up at her. "Yeah. But I'll tell you about it later."

"Okay. Meet me at Fountain Park. I'm leaving right now."

"Is it okay if I go to Mrs. Archer's with Carrie for a little while?" Tina asked her mother.

Mrs. Martell pursed her lips and glanced out the window. "For how long?" she asked. "I don't want you riding your bike in the dark."

"I know," Tina said. "But it won't take long and it's really important. Please?"

Mrs. Martell looked at her for a long moment. Then she nodded. "All right. But don't be late for dinner. And make sure your headlight is on."

"I will."

Tina went outside and picked up her bike. As she rode

toward the park, she thought about what would happen if she told Carrie she wanted to quit Pets, Inc. She wasn't absolutely sure she wanted to quit. But lately, things had been hard.

Carrie was waiting for her by the Revolutionary War statue.

"You are the *best* friend in the whole world," Carrie declared.

Tina couldn't help smiling. "You'd do it for me," she said shyly. "Forget it."

"No way!" Carrie started pedaling. "I'll never forget it. I think you're the best person I ever knew. Honest."

Tina didn't know what to say. She looked around. Dusk was falling. Indian Springs had a late Sunday afternoon feeling to it. A few lights were starting to come on.

After a moment, Tina looked back at Carrie. Carrie was smiling at her.

Tina smiled back. She would never quit Pets, Inc. Not while her best friend was part of it. They could find a way out of their troubles if they just tried hard enough. They had to. For the first time all day, Tina felt hopeful.

"Let's just get it over with," she said in a strong voice. She could see the shedding comb sticking out of Carrie's back pocket.

"Okay."

They pedaled out of the park and turned left without speaking. Before they had gone half a block, they heard a shout.

"Carrie! Tina!"

"Hey, that's Jen," Carrie yelped. She and Tina braked. In a moment, Jenny and Hilary rode up.

"Where're you guys going?" Hilary panted. She pushed her hair out of her face.

"We have to go to Mrs. Archer's," Carrie told them.

"Why?" Jenny sounded surprised.

Instead of answering, Carrie took the comb out of her pocket. "Come with us, okay?" Carrie asked them both.

Jenny and Hilary shared a look, and then they both shrugged. "Okay," Jenny agreed.

Tina breathed a sigh of relief. She had heard the term "safety in numbers," and now she knew what it meant.

A few minutes later they stopped their bikes at the end of Mrs. Archer's driveway.

"Do you think she's home?" Tina whispered. They couldn't see any lights on.

"I don't know," Jenny answered.

"There's no way she'll see us even if she is," Carrie added.

"That's true," Hilary agreed. She looked doubtful. "Well . . . I guess . . ."

Without speaking, Tina quietly rode the rest of the way up the driveway. Carrie and the others followed just behind her. They rested their bikes against the porch railing. They were all making as little noise as possible.

It seemed awfully strange to go to Mrs. Archer's house without seeing Mrs. Archer.

"You guys can stay here if you want," Carrie whispered to her sister and Hilary. They both nodded.

Carrie tugged Tina's hand. "This way." She started tiptoeing around the side of the house.

Tina glanced at the front door again. Then she followed Carrie. The brick path was old and uneven. The tree branches overhead made it like a shadowy tunnel.

Up ahead, Carrie stopped in her tracks. She turned and put one finger up to her lips.

Tina halted.

Silently, Carrie pointed at an upstairs window. A soft lamp was on. Mrs. Archer was home after all.

Carrie tiptoed back to Tina. "Don't make any noise, or the dogs will hear," she whispered into Tina's ear.

Tina nodded quickly. She nudged Carrie to go on. They had to get it over with as fast as possible.

Like two silent shadows, Tina and Carrie inched the rest of the way to the back porch. There was a cardboard box full of newspapers by the steps. Slowly, carefully, Carrie pulled the comb out of her back pocket. Then she put it on top of the newspapers. Tina slowly let out her breath.

"Okay. Let's go," she whispered.

Carrie nodded.

Tina went first. The bumpy path was even darker than before. The bricks were hard to walk on, but Tina went as fast as she could. When she was under the lit window, she held her breath.

Then she tripped on a loose brick.

"OW!" She stumbled and clamped one hand over her mouth.

Inside, Napoleon and Josephine started barking.

Both girls froze. Tina stared at Carrie with wide eyes.

"Come on," Carrie hissed. She brushed past Tina and started running for the bikes.

Tina raced after her, her heart pounding.

"What happened?" Jenny whispered hoarsely as they came running up, scared and out of breath.

The porch light came on. Tina, Carrie, Jenny, and Hilary

were captured in the bright glow. They stood frozen in place.

The door opened. "Who's there?" came Mrs. Archer's voice. The elderly woman stood in the doorway. Josie and Polie were barking happily. "Girls?"

Tina gulped hard and stared at Carrie.

Carrie bit her lip. Jenny let out a soft groan.

Then Carrie smiled up into the light. "Hi, Mrs. Archer."

# 10

"What are you *doing*, girls?" Mrs. Archer asked.

Tina fidgeted awkwardly. "Ummm . . ."

"We didn't know you were home," Carrie explained. "I just brought back the shedding comb I borrowed."

Mrs. Archer beckoned to them. "Well, come on inside." Nobody moved. "Come on," she repeated.

Before anyone could answer, Mrs. Archer turned and went back inside. Napoleon and Josephine looked out at the girls. Their friendly brown eyes were wide and curious.

"What should we do?" Hilary whispered.

Carrie shrugged. "Go in, I guess."

Tina winced. It was going to be so embarrassing. But she followed Carrie, Jenny, and Hilary up the stairs and through the door.

"You know, I've been thinking and thinking all day long," Mrs. Archer was saying to the others when Tina entered the kitchen. She paused. "Come on in, Tina."

Tina sat down obediently at the table, glancing at her friends. She sneaked a quick, worried look at Mrs. Archer's face. But Mrs. Archer had the same twinkly smile she always wore. Tina relaxed a little bit.

"And what I've been thinking," Mrs. Archer continued, "is that I owe you girls an apology."

Tina blinked. "That's okay," she stammered.

"You don't—" Jenny rushed in.

"Now, now. Let me finish," Mrs. Archer said.

Tina bit her lip and looked at Carrie. Carrie looked as uncomfortable as everyone else.

"You're all such nice, sweet girls," Mrs. Archer said. "And I'm afraid I wanted you all to myself." She looked at Tina over the rims of her glasses and smiled sadly. "I guess I was feeling a little hopeless and pitiful."

Nobody had an answer to that. But Mrs. Archer was still smiling. After a moment, Tina smiled back.

"What I need is something to do, something to make me feel useful," Mrs. Archer went on. She shook her head. "A job of some kind."

"A job?" Carrie echoed.

Mrs. Archer pushed her glasses up her nose. "Well, something to do, anyway. Probably some volunteer work to get myself involved with people. But—"

The phone rang.

"Excuse me, girls," Mrs. Archer said. She reached for the telephone and spoke for a few moments. With a smile, she wrote a note on a slip of paper. "Bye, now," she finished and hung up.

As Mrs. Archer finished writing her note, a crazy plan was taking shape in Tina's mind. She swallowed hard. If her plan worked, it would be a miracle! It would solve their problems! But would it work? She turned and looked at Carrie. Her friend was making kissing sounds to Mrs. Archer's lovebirds. Hilary and Jenny were busy petting Polie and Josie.

"Well, now. Where were we?" Mrs. Archer said. "Oh, yes. Something to keep me from being a nuisance to my dear friends."

Tina scooted her chair closer to the table. She felt the same kind of scary excitement she got from jumping off the high dive at the Indian Springs Swim Club. Maybe her plan was crazy, but it was worth a try. She was going to take the chance.

"Would you want to work all the time?" she asked Mrs. Archer quietly.

Mrs. Archer pursed her mouth. "No, not really. Just a couple of hours a day would suit me better, but I'm not sure where I could do something like that."

"Ummm . . ." Tina felt herself blush. She cleared her throat.

Carrie was giving her a questioning look. Jenny wasn't looking at her, but she had a listening expression on her face. Hilary coughed lightly.

"Yes, Tina?" Mrs. Archer said.

Tina twisted her hands together in her lap. "Did you ever think about being . . . like a secretary or . . . or something like that?" she asked in a rush.

"A secretary?" Mrs. Archer looked surprised.

"Sure," Tina said breathlessly. "Like answering the telephone, taking messages, making appointments, stuff like that. You know, for a small, busy company. You might even be able to do it at home."

Carrie let out a tiny yelp of surprise as she realized what Tina meant. Tina kicked her under the table and glanced over at Jenny and Hilary. They were both staring at her in amazement. Carrie scowled at her and bent forward to massage her ankle.

"You could be an organizer for them," Jenny said slowly, catching on. Her serious brown eyes sparkled.

"Well, now, let me see." Mrs. Archer took off her glasses and tapped her chin with her finger. After a moment she smiled. "It sounds right up my alley."

Tina grinned. "And then the people you worked for could come over and get their messages," she added.

"And they could visit you at the same time," Carrie put in. She grinned at her sister.

Mrs. Archer smiled at Tina in a puzzled way. "Tina, you sound like you have something specific in mind. Do you actually *know* someone who needs help like that?"

Tina glanced at Carrie again. They both giggled at the same time.

"Yes, I do," Tina said.

Carrie nodded. "Me, too."

"Me, three," Jenny added.

Hilary had a dreamy expression on her face. "Me, four."

Suddenly a sparkle lit Mrs. Archer's eyes. "As a matter of fact," she said, "I think I do, too."

"And these people wouldn't ever get their calls messed up," Carrie put in. "And that way they could keep their business going."

Mrs. Archer's smile grew brighter. "Exactly! I could be a

lot of help to a business like that." She stood up and went to the telephone. She picked up the receiver and said, "Hello? Pets, Incorporated. May I help you?"

Tina was so happy, her heart felt too big for her body. A shiver of delight ran up her spine.

Mrs. Archer hung up the phone. "Are you sure that's what you want?" she asked the girls.

All four of them nodded at the same time. Tina's eyes were wide with excitement as she turned to the others. "All we'd have to do is make new fliers with Mrs. Archer's number." "And call all our clients," Jenny put in. "But that'll be easy!"

"Yeah," Carrie agreed. She smiled so wide all her teeth showed. "Definitely!"

"And this way, your mothers can have some peace and quiet, and I can have some hustle and bustle," Mrs. Archer said with a laugh.

Napoleon stood up and put his front paws in her lap. Mrs. Archer chuckled. "Tina, I think it's a perfectly marvelous idea."

To Tina's surprise, she felt tears come to her eyes. She felt so much better. It wasn't just having the phone problem straightened out, either. It was having Mrs. Archer for a friend again.

Mrs. Archer reached over and patted her hand. Tina smiled through her tears.

"As president of Pets, Inc., I officially nominate Mrs. Archer to be our chief message taker and organizer," said Jenny. "Everyone votes—"

"I vote yes," Carrie interrupted.

"Me, too," said Hilary.

Tina nodded.

Mrs. Archer beamed. "Then it looks like it's all set."

Tina couldn't wait any longer. She jumped up and threw her arms around Mrs. Archer. She had never hugged someone who wasn't a relative before in her life. But it felt like the right thing to do.

Mrs. Archer hugged her back. "I think you girls should be getting home now. It must be close to dinnertime."

"Okay," Jenny agreed. "Thanks."

The four girls were silent as they rode down the driveway from Mrs. Archer's house. Then Carrie let out a whoop. "It's totally perfect. You're a genius, Tina-bedina."

"No, I'm not," Tina laughed. Darkness was falling fast. She switched on the headlamp on her bike. "I'm just really glad, aren't you guys?"

Carrie nodded. "Definitely."

"Yes," Hilary agreed. Jenny smiled at her in the fading light. They rode two by two down the street.

All of the tiredness and disappointment had disappeared. There was a happy, excited, hopeful feeling in the group. Everything seemed brighter now.

"You know, I was so upset when those ferrets escaped," Tina told Carrie.

Her friend giggled. "You're telling me. I would've died."

"Yeah," Tina went on. "But I found them, right? And I could handle Thor, too." She smiled to herself. "It really wasn't so bad."

*It wasn't so bad*, she repeated silently. None of those things were really disasters in the way she used to think. She had solved those problems on her own. And now she had solved

Pets, Inc.'s, biggest problem of all. She began to think about what else she might accomplish if she tried.

"I can't wait for music class tomorrow," she said to Carrie. Her heart was beating hard.

Carrie zigzagged closer. "Why?"

"I want to ask Mr. Clark something," she giggled, surprised at her own boldness.

Jenny looked back at her. "Like what?"

"Like, maybe I'll invite him over to meet my mom," Tina replied.

Carrie gasped. "You wouldn't!"

"Well . . ." Tina wrinkled her nose. Maybe she wouldn't *really* have the nerve to do it. Then again, she had taken a chance with Mrs. Archer, and it had worked . . . "We'll see," she said.

Carrie was silent for a few seconds. Then she said, "Tina, I'm glad you're my best friend."

"I'm really glad we're all in Pets, Inc.," Hilary added.

"Me, too," Tina agreed. They all braked by the entrance to Fountain Park. That was where they would split up and go their separate ways.

They looked at each other. They were all smiling.

"See you guys tomorrow," said Carrie.

Tina let out a happy sigh. "See you tomorrow."

Then she turned and headed for home.

FOLLOW
THE ADVENTURES
OF IN THE NEXT BOOK,

# Hilary to the Rescue,

## COMING TO YOUR BOOKSTORE SOON.

In *Hilary to the Rescue*, Pets, Inc., gets an exciting new job taking care of the horses at a local stable. Hilary's knowledge about horses proves especially useful when there's a crisis involving one of the girls' charges.

Here's a scene from HILARY TO THE RESCUE:

There was a phone in the garage. Hilary caught her breath while Mr. Crane dialed. She heard him say into the phone.

"Sheriff? Bert Crane up at Stanton Hill. One of our horses is out, might be on the road. Can you send a car to look?" He paused, nodding. "Black Arabian. Right. I'll be here."

After he'd hung up, Hilary reached for the phone. "I'll call my friends," she said. "They can come help." Somehow, she managed to dial Mrs. Archer's number. She closed her eyes and whispered, "Please be there, Jenny. Please."

"Hello?"

Hilary's eyes flew open. "Mrs. Archer! It's Hilary! Is Jenny there, or Carrie or Tina?"

"Why, yes. Jenny just got back from a job. What's wrong?"

Hilary tried not to stumble over her words. "It's Jet—one of the horses at Stanton Hill. She's gotten loose and I need help finding her. Tell Jenny to come over right now!"

"Of course," Mrs. Archer said quickly.

Without waiting to say good-bye, Hilary hung up the phone.

"I told the sheriff I'd stay here and meet the squad car when it comes," Mr. Crane said. "Do you think you can start on your own?"

Hilary coiled the lead rope around her hand. She knew it wouldn't be long before Jenny and the rest of Pets, Inc. arrived, but for now she was on her own. She nodded at Mr. Crane. "I'll find her."

## ABOUT THE AUTHOR

Jennifer Armstrong lives is Saratoga Springs, New York, with a dog named Minch, a cat named Willi, and several tropical fish called The Dudes. She has had dogs, cats, gerbils, mice, parakeets, and fish for pets, but insects give her the creeps. Ms. Armstrong hopes her readers will never be cruel to animals.

# ENTER BANTAM BOOKS'
# PETS INC. PHOTO CONTEST

## OFFICIAL RULES:

1. *No purchase is necessary.* Enter by submitting a black and white or color photograph of your pet in any one of the seven categories listed. Complete the Official Entry Form below (or handprint your name, address, date of birth and the category you are entering on a plain 3"x 5" card) and send both the entry form (or card) and your entry photograph to: **Bantam Books' PETS INC. PHOTO CONTEST, YR Marketing, 666 Fifth Avenue, New York, New York 10103.**

2. Prizes/Seven Ways to Win!
One winning entry will be chosen in each of the seven categories listed below:

**Most Talented Pet**
**Cutest Pet**
**Funniest Looking Pet**
**Biggest Pet**
**Smallest Pet**
**Pet Who Looks Most Like Its Owner**
**Most Unusual Pet**

Each of the seven pet owners who win will be awarded a Polaroid Instant Camera (Approximate Retail Value: $75.00) and each winning pet will receive a yummy treat (Approximate Retail Value $10.00).

3. Contest begins on March 1, 1990. All completed entries must be postmarked and received by Bantam no later than November 15, 1990. All photos must be original. The winning photograph within each category will be judged by the Bantam Marketing Department on the basis of creativity and originality, and Bantam's decisions are final and binding. The winners will be notified by mail on or about January 1, 1991. Winners have 30 days from date of notice in which to accept their prize award or an alternative winner will be chosen. Odds of winning are dependent on the number of entries received. In the event there are an insufficient number of entries that meet the minimum standards established by the judges, Bantam reserves the right not to award all the prizes. Limit one photo per pet entered. All the entry information must be printed on the back of the photo entered. Limit one prize per household or address. If the winner is a minor, prizes will be awarded to and in the name of the pet owner's parent or legal guardian. No prize substitutions or transfers allowed. Bantam is not responsible for lost, incompletely identified or misdirected entries.

4. Prize winners and their parents or legal guardians may be required to execute an Affidavit of Eligibility and Promotional Release supplied by Bantam. Entering the contest constitutes permission for use of each winner's contest submission, name, address and likeness for publicity and promotional purposes, with no additional compensation. All photographs entered become the property of Bantam Books on entry and will not be returned. All photos entered must be original photos that are the sole and exclusive property of the entering owner.

5. Employees of Bantam Books, Bantam Doubleday Dell Publishing Group, Inc., their subsidiaries and affiliates, and their immediate family members are not eligible to enter this contest. This contest is open to residents of the U.S. and Canada, excluding the Province of Quebec. Canadian winners may be required to correctly answer an arithmetical skill-testing question in order to receive their prize. Void where prohibited or restricted by law. All federal, state and local regulations apply. Taxes, if any, are the winner's sole responsibility.

6. For a list of winners, send a stamped, self-addressed envelope entirely separate from your entry to Bantam "Pets Inc. Photo Contest" Winners List, Bantam Books, YR Marketing, 666 Fifth Avenue, New York, New York 10103.

Great FREE offer
just for you!

# Join SNEAK PEEKS™!

Do you want to know what's new before anyone else? Do you like to read great books about girls just like you? If you do, then you won't want to miss SNEAK PEEKS™! Be the first of your friends to know what's hot ... When you join SNEAK PEEKS™, we'll send you FREE inside information in the mail about the latest books ... *before they're published!* Plus updates on your favorite series, authors, and exciting new stories filled with friendship and fun ... adventure and mystery ... girlfriends and boyfriends.

It's easy to be a member of SNEAK PEEKS™. Just fill out the coupon below ... and get ready for fun! It's FREE! Don't delay—sign up today!